THE COMPLETE
MOTHER GOOSE

publications international, ltd.

Cover, title page, and table of contents illustrated by Dan Andreasen

Illustrations by:
Martha Avilés, Lisa Berrett, Bill Bolton, Krista Brauckmann-Towns,
Drew Brook-Cormack Associates, Nan Brooks, Sharon Cartwright, Linda Clearwater, Carolyn Croll,
Betsy Day, Wendy Edelson, Amanda Enright, Lori Nelson Field, Jon Goodell, Kate Sturman Gorman,
Martin Irish, Thea Kliros, Astrid Kroemer, Judith Dufour Love, Tammie Lyon, Ben Mahan, Anastasia Mitchell,
Margie Moore, Robin Moro, Anita Nelson, Kathleen O'Malley, Wayne Parmenter, Debbie Pinkney,
Karen Pritchett, Susan Spellman, Jeremy Tugeau, Rosario Valderrama, and Maria Woods

Louis Weber, C.E.O., Publications International, Ltd.
7373 North Cicero Avenue, Lincolnwood, Illinois 60712

Ground Floor, 59 Gloucester Place, London W1U 8JJ

Customer Service: 1-800-595-8484 or customer_service@pilbooks.com

www.pilbooks.com

Permission is never granted for commercial purposes.

p i kids is a registered trademark of Publications International, Ltd.

8 7 6 5 4 3 2 1

ISBN-13: 978-1-4127-5927-4
ISBN-10: 1-4127-5927-7

Table of Contents

Old MacDonald's Farm

The Learned Pig

My learned friend and neighbor pig,
Odds bobs and bills, and dash my wig!
It's said that you the weather know.
Please tell me when the wind will blow.

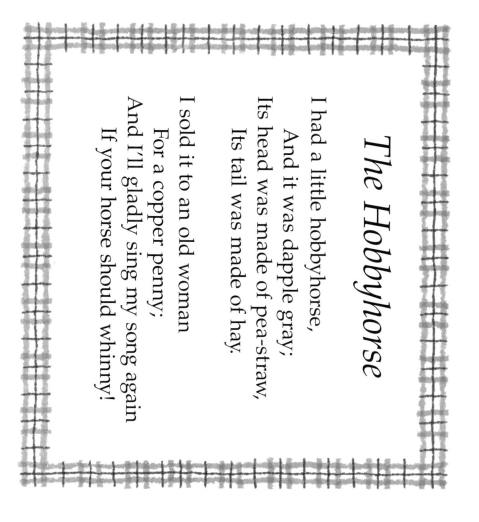

The Hobbyhorse

I had a little hobbyhorse,
  And it was dapple gray;
Its head was made of pea-straw,
  Its tail was made of hay.

I sold it to an old woman
  For a copper penny;
And I'll gladly sing my song again
  If your horse should whinny!

The Piper and His Cow

There was a piper had a cow,
Though he had nothing to give her;
Pulled out his pipes and played a tune,
And asked the cow to consider.

The cow considered very well,
And gave the piper some money,
And asked him to play another tune
That she would find quite funny.

Shave a Pig

Barber, barber, shave a pig,
How many hairs will make a wig?
Four-and-twenty, that's enough,
Give the barber a pinch of snuff.

There Was a Little Pig

There was a little pig,
Who wasn't very big,
So they put him in a great big show.

While playing in the band,
He broke his little hand,
And now he can't play his old banjo.

The Donkey

Donkey, donkey, old and gray,
Open your mouth and gently bray;
Lift your ears and blow your horn,
To wake the world this sleepy morn.

Charlie Warlie

Charlie Warlie had a cow,
Black and white around the brow;
Open the gate and let her in,
Charlie's cow is home again.

Robert Barnes

Robert Barnes, fellow fine,
Can you shoe this horse of mine?
Yes, good sir, that I can,
As well as any other man.
There's a nail, and there's a prod,
And now, good sir, your horse is shod.

A Horse and a Flea

A horse and a flea
    and three blind mice
Met each other
    while skating on ice.
The horse he slipped
    and fell on the flea.
The flea said, "Oops!
    There's a horse on me!"

Old MacDonald

Old MacDonald had a farm, *E-I-E-I-O.*
On his farm he had some cows, *E-I-E-I-O.*
With a moo-moo here and a moo-moo there,
Here a moo, there a moo, everywhere a moo-moo.

Old MacDonald had a farm, *E-I-E-I-O.*
On his farm he had some donkeys, *E-I-E-I-O.*
With a hee-haw here and a hee-haw there,
Here a hee, there a haw,
everywhere a hee-haw.

Old MacDonald had a farm, *E-I-E-I-O*.
On this farm he had some pigs, *E-I-E-I-O*.
With an oink-oink here and an oink-oink there,
Here an oink, there an oink,
     everywhere an oink-oink.

Old MacDonald had a farm, *E-I-E-I-O*.
On this farm he had some ducks, *E-I-E-I-O*.
With a quack-quack here and a quack-quack there,
Here a quack, there a quack,
     everywhere a quack-quack.

Old MacDonald had a farm,
     E-I-E-I-O.

Cock-a-Doodle-Doo

Cock-a-doodle-doo,

My dame has lost her shoe,

And master's lost his fiddling stick,

Sing doodle-doodle-doo.

Upon My Word

Upon my word and honor

As I went to Bonner,

I met a pig

Without a wig,

Upon my word and honor.

The Little Mouse

I have seen you, little mouse,
    Running all about the house.
Through the hole your little eye
    In the wainscot, peeping sly.
Hoping soon some crumbs to steal,
    To make quite a hearty meal.
Look before you venture out,
    See if kitty is about.

Mary Had a Little Lamb

Mary had a little lamb,
Its fleece was white as snow.
And everywhere that Mary went,
The lamb was sure to go.

Baa, Baa, Black Sheep

Baa, baa, black sheep,
Have you any wool?
Yes, sir. Yes, sir.
Three bags full.
One for the master,
One for the dame,
And one for the little boy
Who lives down the lane.
Baa, baa, black sheep,
Have you any wool?
Yes, sir. Yes, sir.
Three bags full.

A Dozen Eggs

I bought a dozen new-laid eggs

From good old Farmer Dickens.

I hobbled home upon two legs

And found them full of chickens.

Three Blind Mice

Three blind mice, three blind mice.
See how they run, see how they run!
They all ran after the poor farmer's wife,
Who has been afraid of mice all her life.
Did you ever think you'd see such a sight,
As three blind mice that create such a fright?

Three blind mice.

Harvesting

The boughs do shake
And the bells do ring,
So merrily comes our harvest in,
Our harvest in, our harvest in,
So merrily comes our harvest in.

We've plowed, we've sowed,
We've reaped, we've mowed,
We've got our harvest in.

Calendar Rhymes

March Winds

March winds
And April showers
Bring forth May flowers.

Thirty Days
Hath September

Thirty days hath September,
April, June, and November;
February has twenty-eight alone.
All the rest have thirty-one,
Excepting leap year — that's the time
When February has twenty-nine.

Play Days

How many days has my baby to play?
Saturday, Sunday, Monday,
Tuesday, Wednesday, Thursday, Friday;
Saturday, Sunday, Monday,
Hop away, skip away,
My baby wants to play.
My baby wants to play every day.

Calm in June

Calm weather in June
Sets corn in tune.

The Greedy Man

The greedy man is he who sits
And bites bits out of plates,
Or else takes up a calendar
And gobbles all the dates.

Saturday, Sunday

On Saturday night
Shall be all my care
To powder my locks
And curl my hair.

On Sunday morning
My love will come in,
When he will marry me
With a gold ring.

After Sunday

As Tommy Snooks and Bessy Brooks

Were walking out one Sunday,

Says Tommy Snooks to Bessy Brooks,

"Tomorrow will be Monday."

Winter

Cold and raw the north wind doth blow,
Bleak in the morning early.
All the hills are covered with snow,
And winter's now come fairly.

When the Snow
Is on the Ground

The little robin grieves
When the snow is on the ground.
For the trees have no leaves,
And no berries can be found.
So toss the robin some bread or cheese,
And then he'll eat till spring comes round.

A Week of Birthdays

Monday's child is fair of face,
Tuesday's child is full of grace,
Wednesday's child is full of woe,
Thursday's child has far to go,
Friday's child is loving and giving,
Saturday's child works hard for its living,
But the child born on the Sabbath day,
Is bonny and blithe, and good and gay.

Silly People Rhymes

Mary, Mary

Mary, Mary, quite contrary,
How does your garden grow?
With silver bells and cockleshells,
And pretty maids all in a row.

Handy Pandy

Handy Pandy, Jack-a-dandy,
Loves plum cake and sugar candy.

He bought some at a grocer's shop,
And out he came—hop, hop, hop.

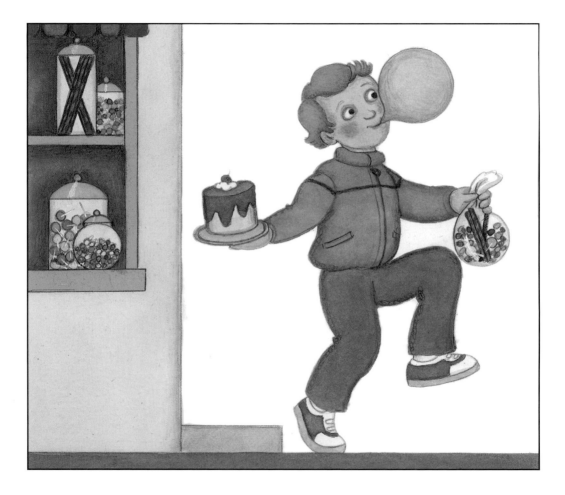

The House that Jack Built

This is the house that Jack built.
This is the malt that lay
In the house that Jack built.

This is the rat that ate the malt,
That lay in the house that Jack built.

This is the cat that killed the rat,
That ate the malt in the house that Jack built.

This is the dog that worried the cat,
That killed the rat that ate the malt,
That lay in the house that Jack built.

This is the cow with the crumpled horn,
That tossed the dog that worried the cat,
That killed the rat that ate the malt,
That lay in the house that Jack built.

This is the maiden all forlorn,
That milked the cow
        with the crumpled horn,
That tossed the dog that worried the cat,
That killed the rat that ate the malt,
That lay in the house that Jack built.

This is the man all tattered and torn,
That kissed the maiden all forlorn,
That milked the cow with the crumpled horn,
That tossed the dog that worried the cat…

That killed the rat that ate the malt,
That lay in the house that Jack built.

This is the priest all shaven and shorn,
That married the man
       all tattered and torn,
That kissed the maiden all forlorn,
That milked the cow
       with the crumpled horn,

That tossed the dog that worried the cat,
That killed the rat that ate the malt,
That lay in the house that Jack built.

This is the farmer sowing his corn,
That kept the rooster that crowed in the morn,
That waked the priest all shaven and shorn,

That married the man
       all tattered and torn,
That kissed the maiden all forlorn,
That milked the cow
       with the crumpled horn,

That tossed the dog that worried the cat,
That killed the rat that ate the malt,
That lay in the house that Jack built.

Peter White

Peter White will ne'er go right,
And would you know the reason why?
He follows his nose wherever he goes,
And all that stands awry.

The Piper's Son

Tom, Tom, the piper's son,
Stole a pig and away he run!
The pig thought it was quite a treat,
To be carried down the street.

Nothing-at-All

There was an old woman called Nothing-at-all,
Who lived in a dwelling exceedingly small;
A man stretched his mouth to the utmost extent,
And down in one gulp,
the house and old woman went.

Miss Mackay

Alas, alas, for Miss Mackay!
Her knives and forks have run away.
And where the cups and spoons are going,
She's sure there is no way of knowing.

Anna Elise

Anna Elise,
She jumped with surprise.
The surprise was so quick,
It played her a trick.
The trick was so rare,
She jumped in a chair.
The chair was so frail,
She jumped in a pail,
The pail was so wet,
She jumped in a net.

The net was so small,
She jumped on a ball.
The ball was so round,
She jumped on the ground.
And ever since then
She's been turning around.

The Old Woman

The old woman stands
at the tub, tub, tub,
The dirty clothes
to rub, rub, rub;
But when they are clean
and fit to be seen,
She'll dress like a lady
and dance on the green.

Rub-a-Dub-Dub

Rub-a-dub-dub,
Three men in a tub,
And how do you think they got there?
The butcher, the baker,
The candlestick maker,
They all jumped out of a rotten potato,
'Twas enough to make a man stare.

The Old Woman Under the Hill

There was an old woman
Lived under a hill;
And if she's not gone,
She lives there still.

Moses' Toeses

Moses supposes his toeses are roses,
But Moses supposes erroneously.
For nobody's toeses are posies of roses
As Moses supposes his toeses to be.

If Wishes Were Horses

If wishes were horses,
Beggars would ride.
If turnips were watches,
I would wear one by my side.
And if "ifs" and "ands"
Were pots and pans,
There'd be no work for tinkers!

Lock and Key

"I am a gold lock."
"I am a gold key."
"I am a silver lock."
"I am a silver key."
"I am a brass lock."
"I am a brass key."
"I am a lead lock."
"I am a lead key."
"I am a don lock."
"I am a don key!"

Three Wise Men

Three wise men of Gotham
Went to sea in a bowl.

If the bowl had been stronger,
My song would be longer.

Solomon Grundy

Solomon Grundy,
Born on Monday,
Christened on Tuesday,
Married on Wednesday,
Took ill on Thursday,
Worse on Friday,
Died on Saturday,
Buried on Sunday.
This is the end of Solomon Grundy.

Gregory Griggs

Gregory Griggs, Gregory Griggs,
Had twenty-seven different wigs.
He wore them up, he wore them down,
To please the people of the town.
He wore them east, he wore them west,
And never could tell
Which one he liked best.

Tweedle-dum and Tweedle-dee

Tweedle-dum and Tweedle-dee
Resolved to have a battle.
For Tweedle-dum said Tweedle-dee
Had spoiled his nice new rattle.

Just then flew by a monstrous crow,
As big as a tar barrel.
Which frightened both the heroes so,
They quite forgot their quarrel.

Play-Along Rhymes

Swim

Mother, may I go out to swim?
Yes, my darling daughter.
Hang your clothes on a hickory limb
And don't go near the water.

Here We Go Round the Mulberry Bush

Here we go round the mulberry bush,
The mulberry bush,
The mulberry bush.
Here we go round the mulberry bush,
On a cold and frosty morning.

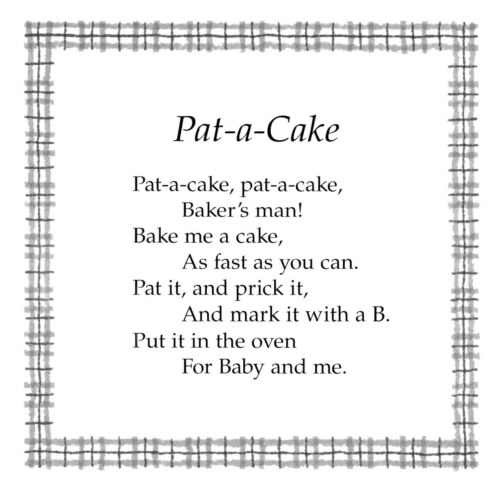

Pat-a-Cake

Pat-a-cake, pat-a-cake,
    Baker's man!
Bake me a cake,
    As fast as you can.
Pat it, and prick it,
    And mark it with a B.
Put it in the oven
    For Baby and me.

Rain, Rain, Go Away

Rain, rain, go away,

Come again another day;

Little Johnny wants to play.

Billy, Billy

Billy, Billy, come and play,
While the sun shines bright as day.
Yes, my Polly, so I will,
For I love to please you still.
Billy, Billy, have you seen
Sam and Betsy on the green?
Yes, my dear, I saw them pass,
Skipping over the new-mown grass.

Georgie Porgie

Georgie Porgie, pudding and pie,
Kissed the girls and made them cry.
When the boys came out to play,
Georgie Porgie ran away.

Come Out to Play

Girls and boys,
Come out to play.
The moon doth shine
As bright as day.
Leave your supper,
And leave your sleep,
Come and play with your pals,
Out in the street.

This Little Piggy

This little piggy went to market.
This little piggy stayed home.
This little piggy had roast beef.
This little piggy had none.
This little piggy cried,
"Wee-wee-wee!"
All the way home.

Little Boys and Girls

Patience Is a Virtue

Patience is a virtue,
Virtue is a grace;
Grace is a little girl
Who wouldn't wash her face.

Little Jack Horner

Little Jack Horner
Sat in a corner
Eating his Christmas pie;

He put in his thumb,
And pulled out a plum,
And cried, "What a good boy am I!"

There Was a Little Girl

The was a little girl who had a little curl,
Right in the middle of her forehead.
And when she was good, she was very, very good,
But when she was bad, she was horrid.

She stood on her head on her little trundle bed,
With no one there to say "no."
She screamed and she squalled, she yelled and she bawled,
And drummed her little heels against the window.

Her mother heard the noise, and thought it was the toys,
Falling in the dusty attic.
She rushed up the flight, and saw she was alright,
And hugged her most emphatic.

Freddie and the Cherry Tree

Freddie saw some fine ripe cherries
Hanging on a cherry tree.
And he said, "You pretty cherries,
Will you not come down to me?"

"Thank you kindly," said a cherry,
"We would rather stay up here;
If we ventured down this morning,
You would eat us up, I fear."

One, the finest of the cherries,
Dangled from a slender twig.
"You are beautiful," said Freddie,
"Red and ripe, and oh, how big!"

"Catch me!" said the cherry. "Catch me,
Little master, if you can."
"I would catch you very soon," said Freddie,
"If I were a grown-up man."

Freddie jumped, and tried to reach it,
Standing high upon his toes;
But the cherry bobbed about,
And laughed, and tickled Freddie's nose.

"Never mind," said little Freddie,
"I shall have them when it's right."
But a blackbird whistled boldly,
"I shall have them all tonight."

Dirty Jim

There was one little Jim,
'Tis reported of him,
And must be to his lasting disgrace,
That he never was seen
With hands at all clean,
Nor yet ever clean was his face.

His friends were much hurt
To see so much dirt,
And often they made him quite clean;
But all was in vain,
He got dirty again,
And not at all fit to be seen.

It gave him no pain
To hear them complain,
Nor his own dirty clothes to survey;
His indolent mind
No pleasure could find
In tidy and wholesome array.

Though unkempt and messy,
Unlike his friend Jessie,
Jim loved dirty ways to be sure;
But neat kids are seen,
To be decent and clean,
And their smiles are ever so pure.

Little Miss Muffet

Little Miss Muffet
Sat on a tuffet,
Eating her curds and whey.

There came a big spider,
Who sat down beside her
And frightened Miss Muffet away.

My Little Brother

Little brother, darling boy,
You are very dear to me!
I am happy—full of joy,
When your smiling face I see.

How I wish that you could speak,
And could know the words I say!
Pretty stories I would seek,
To amuse you every day.

Shake your rattle, here it is,
Listen to its merry noise;
And when you are tired of this,
I will bring you other toys.

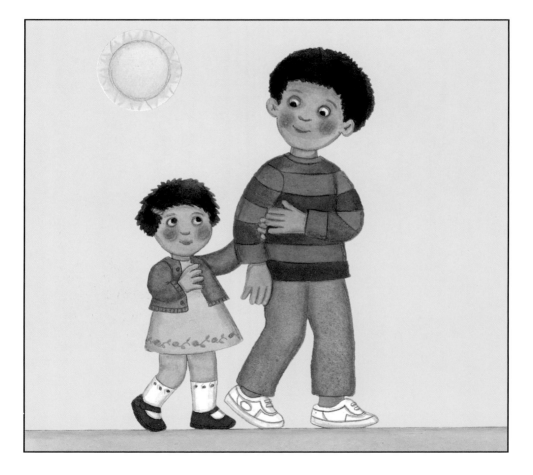

My Little Sister

I have a little sister,
She is only two years old;
But to us at home who love her,
She is worth her weight in gold.

We often play together,
And I begin to find,
That to make my sister happy,
I must be very kind.

I must not taunt or tease her,
Or ever angry be
With the darling little sister
That God has given to me.

Jack Jelf

Little Jack Jelf
Was put upon a shelf
Because he could not spell "pie";

When his aunt, Mrs. Grace,
Saw his sorrowful face,
She could not help saying, "Oh, my!"

Little Polly Flinders

Little Polly Flinders,
Sat among the cinders,
Warming her pretty little toes;
Her mother came and stopped her,
For fear her lovely daughter
Would toast her pretty little nose.

Busy-Time Rhymes

To Market

To market, to market, to buy a fat pig;
　　Home again, home again, jiggety-jig.
To market, to market, to buy a fat hog;
　　Home again, home again, jiggety-jog.

Willy Boy

Willy boy, Willy boy,
Where are you going?
I will go with you,
If that I may.

I'm going to the meadow,
To see them a-mowing;
I'm going to help them,
To make the hay.

The Old Woman of Leeds

There was an old
Woman of Leeds,
Who spent her time
In good deeds.

She worked for the poor
Till her fingers were sore,
This pious old
Woman of Leeds!

Peter Piper

Peter Piper picked a peck
Of pickled peppers;
A peck of pickled peppers
Peter Piper picked.

If Peter Piper picked a peck
Of pickled peppers,
Where's the peck of pickled peppers
Peter Piper picked?

Sweep

Sweep, sweep, chimney sweep,

From the bottom to the top.

Sweep it all up, chimney sweep,

From the bottom to the top.

Jack and Jill

Jack and Jill went up the hill,
To fetch a pail of water.
Jack fell down and broke his crown,
And Jill came tumbling after.

Up Jack got and home did trot,
As fast as he could caper.
He went to bed to mend his head
With vinegar and brown paper.

I Love You Rhymes

Molly, My Sister

Molly, my sister, and I fell out,
And what do you think it was all about?
She loved coffee and I loved tea,
And that was the reason we couldn't agree.

Lavender Blue

Lavender blue and rosemary green,
When I am king you shall be queen.

Call up my maids at four o'clock,
Some to the wheel and some to the rock.

Some to make hay and some to shear corn,
And you and I will sing until morn.

A Fish for You

There once was a fish.
(What more could you wish?)
He lived in the sea.
(Where else would he be?)
He was caught on a line.
(Whose line if not mine?)
So I brought him to you.
(What else should I do?)

Why May I Not Love Jenny

Jenny shall have a new bonnet,
And Jenny shall go to the fair,
And Jenny shall have a blue ribbon,
To tie up her bonny brown hair.

And why may I not love Jenny?
And why may not Jenny love me?
And why may I not love Jenny,
As well as another body?

Fiddle-De-Dee

Fiddle-de-dee, fiddle-de-dee,
The fly shall marry the bumblebee.
They went to church, and married was she;
The fly had married the bumblebee.

I Love Coffee

I love coffee,
I love tea,
I love the girls,
And they love me.

Boy and Girl

There was a little boy and a little girl
     Lived in an alley;
Says the little boy to the little girl,
     "Shall I, oh, shall I?"
Says the little girl to the little boy,
     "What shall we do?"
Says the little boy to the little girl,
     "I will kiss you."

He Loves Me

He loves me. He don't!
He'll have me. He won't!
He would if he could.
But he can't. So he don't.

Curly Locks

Curly Locks, Curly Locks, will you be mine?
You will not wash dishes nor feed the swine,
But sit on a cushion and sew a fine seam,
And feed upon strawberries, sugar, and cream.

Riddle
Rhymes

Nanny Etticoat

Little Nanny Etticoat,
With a white petticoat
And a red nose;
The longer she stands,
The shorter she grows.

What is she?
A candle.

Going to St. Ives

As I was going to St. Ives,
I met a man with seven wives.
Every wife had seven sacks.
Every sack had seven cats.
Every cat had seven kits.
Kits, cats, sacks, and wives,
How many were going to St. Ives?

Answer:
One.

Elizabeth

Elizabeth, Lizzy, Betsy, and Bess,
They all went together to seek a bird's nest.
They found a bird's nest with five eggs in,
If they all took one out,
How many were in?

Answer:
Four

Winter Blossom

Lives in winter,
Dies in summer,
And grows with its roots upward!

What is it?
An icicle.

Riddle Me This

Riddle me, riddle me,
what is that?

Over the head
and under the hat?

What is this?
Hair.

Fashion Seasons

In spring I look gay,
Decked in comely array.
In summer more clothing I wear.

When colder it grows,
I fling off my clothes,
And in winter quite naked appear.

What is it?
A tree.

A Recipe Riddle

Flour of England, fruit of Spain,
Met together in a shower of rain.
Put in a bag tied round with a string.

If you'll tell me this riddle,
I'll give you a ring.

What is it?
Plum pudding.

Feathered Friends

The Wise Old Owl

A wise old owl sat in an oak.
The more he heard, the less he spoke;
The less he spoke, the more he heard.
Why aren't we all like that wise old bird?

The Brown Thrush

There's a merry brown thrush
Sitting up in the tree.
She's singing to me! She's singing to me!
And what does she say, little girl, little boy?
"Oh, the world's running over with joy!
Don't you hear? Don't you see?
Hush! Look! In my tree,
I'm as happy as can be!"

Answer to a Child's Question

Do you ask what the birds say? The robin, the dove,
The linnet, and thrush say, "I love and I love!"
In the winter they are silent—the wind is so strong;
What it says, I don't know, but it sings a loud song.
But green leaves, and blossoms,
and sunny warm weather,
And singing, and loving—all come back together.
But the lark is so brimful of gladness and love,
The green fields below him, the blue sky above,
That he sings, and he sings, and forever sings he:
"I love my love, and my love loves me."

The Canary

Mary had a little bird,
With feathers bright and yellow,
Slender legs—upon my word,
He was a pretty fellow.

Sweetest notes he always sung,
Which much delighted Mary;
Often when his cage was hung,
She sat to hear Canary.

The Duck

Behold the duck.
It does not cluck.
A cluck it lacks.
It quacks.
'Tis especially fond
Of a puddle or pond.
When it dines or sups,
It bottoms up.

The Robin

When up aloft I fly and fly,
I see in pools the shining sky,

And a happy bird
Am I, am I!

The Owl and the Pussycat

The owl and the pussycat went to sea
In a beautiful pea-green boat.
They took some honey, and plenty of money,
Wrapped up in a five-pound note.
The owl looked up to the stars above,
And sang to a small guitar,
"O lovely Pussy! O Pussy, my love,
What a beautiful Pussy you are, you are, you are!
What a beautiful Pussy you are!"

Pussy said to the owl, "You elegant fowl!
How charmingly sweet you sing!
O let us be married! Too long have we tarried,
But what shall we do for a ring?"

They sailed away for a year and a day,
To the land where the Bong-tree grows,
And there in a wood a Piggy-wig stood,
With a ring at the end of his nose, his nose,
With a ring at the end of his nose.

"Dear Pig, are you willing to sell for one shilling
Your ring?" Said the Piggy, "I will."
So they took it away and were married next day
By the turkey who lives on the hill.
They dined on mince, and slices of quince,
Which they ate with a runcible spoon;
And hand in hand, on the edge of the sand,
They danced by the light of the moon,
They danced by the light of the moon.

Time to Rise

A birdie with a yellow bill
Hopped upon the window sill,
Tipped his shining eye, and said:
"Aren't you ashamed, you sleepyhead?"

The North Wind
Doth Blow

The north wind doth blow,
And we shall have snow,
And what will the robin do then,
poor thing?
He'll sit in a barn
And keep himself warm,
And hide his head under his wing.

The Owl

When cats run home and light is come,
 And the dew is cold upon the ground,
And the far-off stream is dumb,
 And the whirring sail goes round,
And the whirring sail goes round,
 Alone and warming his five wits,
The white owl in the belfry sits.

When the merry milkmaids click the latch,
 And sweetly smells the new-mown hay,
And the rooster sings beneath the thatch,
 Twice or thrice his roundelay;
Twice or thrice his roundelay;
 Alone and warming his five wits,
The white owl in the belfry sits.

Robin Redbreast

Little Robin Redbreast
Sat upon a tree.
Up went Pussycat;
Down went he.
Down came Pussycat;
Away Robin ran.
Says little Robin Redbreast,
"Catch me if you can!"

Counting Rhymes

Three Young Rats

Three young rats with black felt hats,
Three young ducks with white straw flats,
Three young dogs with curling tails,
Three young cats with demi-veils,
Went out to walk with two young pigs
In satin vests and sorrel wigs.
But suddenly it chanced to rain,
And so they all went home again.

One, Two, Buckle My Shoe

One, two, buckle my shoe.
Three, four, knock at the door.
Five, six, pick up sticks.
Seven, eight, lay them straight.
Nine, ten, a good fat hen.

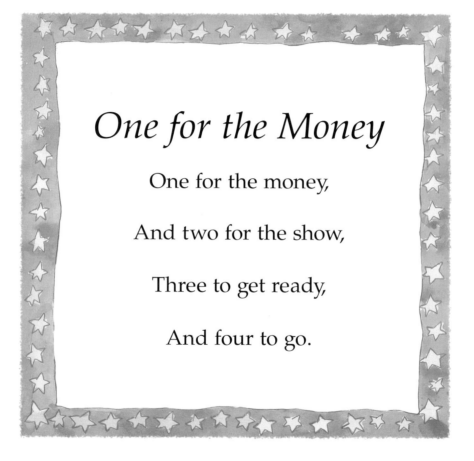

One for the Money

One for the money,

And two for the show,

Three to get ready,

And four to go.

Hot Cross Buns

Hot cross buns! Hot cross buns!
One a penny, two a penny,
Hot cross buns!

If you have no daughters,
Give them to your sons;
One a penny, two a penny,
Hot cross buns!

One, Two, Three

One, two, three, four, five,
Once I caught a fish alive.
Six, seven, eight, nine, ten,
But I let it go again.
Why did you let it go?
Because it bit my finger so.
Which finger did it bite?
The little one upon the right.

Three Little Kittens

Three little kittens,
They lost their mittens,
And they began to cry,
"Oh, mother dear, we sadly fear
That we have lost our mittens."

"Oh dear, don't fear,
My little kittens.
Come in and have some pie."

Yummy Rhymes

Goober and I

Goober and I were baked in a pie,
And it was wonderful hot.
We had nothing to pay
The baker that day
So we crept out and ran away.

Pease Porridge Hot

Pease porridge hot,
Pease porridge cold,
Pease porridge in the pot
Nine days old.
Some like it hot,
Some like it cold,
Some like it in the pot,
Nine days old.

Polly, Put the Kettle On

Polly, put the kettle on,
Polly, put the kettle on,
Polly, put the kettle on, we'll all have tea.

Sukey, take it off again,
Sukey, take it off again,
Sukey, take it off again,
They've all gone away.

Start the fire and make the toast,
Put the muffins down to roast,
Start the fire and make the toast,
We'll all have tea.

Up in the Green Orchard

Up in the green orchard
There is a green tree,
The finest of apples
That you ever did see.
The apples are ripe,
And ready to fall,
And Reuben and Robin
Shall gather them all.

Little Miss Tucket

Little Miss Tucket
 Sat on a bucket,
Eating some peaches and cream.
 There came a grasshopper
Who tried hard to stop her,
 But she said,
  "Go away, or I'll scream!"

An Apple a Day

An apple a day
Sends the doctor away.

Apple in the morning,
Doctor's warning.

Roast apple at night,
Starves the doctor outright.

Eat an apple going to bed,
Knock the doctor on the head.

Three each day, seven days a week,
Rosy apple, rosy cheek.

When Jack's a Very Good Boy

When Jack's a very good boy,
He shall have cakes and custard;
But when he does nothing but cry,
He shall have nothing but mustard.

Green Cheese

Green cheese, yellow laces,
Up and down the marketplaces;
Turn, cheeses, turn.

On Christmas Eve

On Christmas Eve I turned the spit;
I burnt my fingers, I feel it yet.
The sparrow it flew right over the table,
The pot began to play with the ladle;
The ladle stood up like an angry man,
And vowed he'd fight the frying pan.
The frying pan hid behind the door,
Said he never saw the like before;
And the kitchen clock I was going to wind,
Said he never saw the like behind.

Betty Botter

Betty Botter bought some butter,
But, she said, the butter's bitter;
If I put it in my batter,
It will make my batter bitter,
But a bit of better butter
Will make my batter better.
So she bought a bit of butter,
Better than her bitter butter,
And she put it in her batter,
And the batter was not bitter.
So it was better Betty Botter bought
A bit of better butter.

Favorite Rhymes

Old King Cole

Old King Cole
Was a merry old soul,
And a merry old soul was he;
He called for his pipe,
And he called for his bowl,
And he called for his fiddlers three.

Sing a Song of Sixpence

Sing a song of sixpence,
A pocket full of rye;
Four-and-twenty blackbirds
Baked in a pie!

When the pie was opened,
The birds began to sing!
Wasn't that a dainty dish
To set before the king?

Peter Pumpkin-Eater

Peter, Peter, pumpkin-eater,
Had a wife and couldn't keep her.
He put her in a pumpkin shell,
And there he kept her very well.

Old Mother Hubbard

Old Mother Hubbard
Went to the cupboard
To give her poor dog a bone.

When she got there,
The cupboard was bare,
And so her poor dog had none.

222

Old Mother Goose

Old Mother Goose,
When she wanted to wander,
Would ride through the air
On a very fine gander.

There Was an Old Woman

There was an old woman
Who lived in a shoe.
She had so many children,
She didn't know what to do.
She gave them some broth
Without any bread.
She kissed them all sweetly
And sent them to bed.

Jack Sprat

Jack Sprat could eat no fat.
His wife could eat no lean.
And so between them both, you see,
They licked the platter clean.

Humpty Dumpty

Humpty Dumpty sat on a wall;
Humpty Dumpty had a great fall!
All the king's horses
And all the kings men
Couldn't put Humpty together again.

Little Bo-Peep

Little Bo-Peep has lost her sheep,
And can't tell where to find them.
Leave them alone,
And they'll come home,
Wagging their tails behind them.

Puppy Tales

Hark, Hark

Hark, hark, the dogs do bark!
Beggars are coming to town.
Some in jags, and some in rags,
And some in velvet gown.

Where Has My Little Dog Gone?

Oh, where, oh, where
has my little dog gone?
Oh, where, oh, where can he be?
With his ears cut short
and his tail cut long,
Oh, where, oh, where can he be?

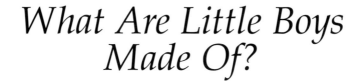

What Are Little Boys Made Of?

What are little boys made of, made of?
What are little boys made of?
Snips and snails and puppy-dog tails;
That's what little boys are made of.

What are little girls made of, made of?
What are little girls made of?
Sugar and spice, and all things nice,
That's what little girls are made of.

My Dog Spot

I have a white dog whose name is Spot,
And he's sometimes white and he's sometimes not.
But whether he's white or whether he's not,
There's a patch on his ear that makes him Spot.

He has a tongue that is long and pink,
And he lolls it out when he wants to think.
He seems to think most when the weather is hot;
He's a wise sort of dog, is my dog, Spot.

He likes a bone and he likes a ball,
But he doesn't care for a cat at all.
He waggles his tail and he knows what's what,
So I'm glad that he's my dog. My dog, Spot.

239

Bow-Wow

Bow-wow, says the dog;
Mew-mew, says the cat;
Grunt, grunt, goes the hog;
And squeak, goes the rat.

Chirp, chirp, says the sparrow;
Caw, caw, says the crow;
Quack, quack, says the duck;
And what cuckoos say, you know.

So, with sparrows and cuckoos,
With rats and with dogs,
With ducks and with crows,
With cats and with hogs,

A fine song I have made,
To please you, mommy dear;
And if it is well sung,
'Twill be charming to hear.

Mother Quack's Dog & Cat

Old Mother Quack lived in a shack
Along with her dog and cat;
What they ate I can't tell
but it's known very well,
That not one of the party was fat.

Old Mother Quack scoured out her shack,
And washed both her dog and cat;
The cat scratched her nose,
And no one quite knows,
Who was the gainer by that?

I'm Just a Little Puppy

I'm just a little puppy
And as good as can be,
And why they call me naughty
I'm sure I cannot see.
I've only carried off one shoe
And torn the baby's hat,
And chased the ducks,
And spilled the milk —
There's nothing bad in that!

Leg Over Leg

Leg over leg,

As the dog went to Dover;

When he came to a fence,

Jump, he went over.

Colorful
Rhymes

Jolly Red Nose

Nose, nose, jolly red nose,
And what gave you
That jolly red nose?
Nutmeg and ginger,
Cinnamon and cloves,
That's what gave me this jolly red nose.

Little Boy Blue

Little Boy Blue,
Come blow your horn.
The sheep's in the meadow,
The cow's in the corn.

Where's the little boy
Who looks after the sheep?
He's under the haystack
Fast asleep.

Gray Goose

Gray goose and gander,

Waft your wings together

And carry the king's daughter

Over the one-strand river.

My Little Pink

My little Pink,
I suppose you think
I cannot do without you.
I'll let you know before I go
How I will fare without you.

Roses Are Red

Roses are red,
Violets are blue,
Sugar is sweet,
And so are you!

Blue Ribbon

If you love me, love me true,
Send me a ribbon, and let it be blue;
If you do not, let it be seen,
Send me a ribbon, a ribbon of green.

The Purple Cow

I never saw a purple cow,
I hope I never see one;
But I can tell you, anyhow,
I'd rather see than be one.

The Brown Owl

The brown owl sits in the ivy bush,
And she looks wondrous wise,
With a horny beak beneath her cowl,
And a pair of large round eyes.

Little Gray Horse

John Cook had a little gray horse;
Hee, haw, hum.
When riding he went back and forth;
Hee, haw, hum.

Kitten Yarns

Dame Trot

Dame Trot and her cat
Sat down for to chat;
The Dame sat on this side,
And Kitty on the mat.

"Kitty," says the Dame,
"Can you catch a rat
Or a mouse in the dark?"
"Purr," says the cat.

The Kilkenny Cats

There were once two cats of Kilkenny,
Each thought there was one cat too many;
So they fought and they fit,
And they scratched and they bit,
Till, excepting their nails
And the tips of their tails,
Instead of two cats, there weren't any.

Ho! My Kitten

Ho! My kitten, a kitten,
And ho! My kitten, my deary!
Such a sweet pet as this
Was neither far nor neary.

Here we go up, up, up,
Here we go down, down, down,
Here we go backward and forward,
And here we go round, round, round.

Little Kitty

I like little kitty,
Her coat is so warm,
And if I don't tease her
She'll do me no harm;
So I'll not pull her tail,
Nor drive her away,
But kitty and I
Very gently will play.

The Quarrelsome Kittens

Two little kittens one stormy night,
They began to quarrel, they began to fight;
One had a mouse and the other had none,
And that's the way the quarrel begun.

"I'll have that mouse," said the biggest cat.
"You'll have that mouse? We'll see about that!"
"I will have that mouse," said the eldest son.
"You shan't have the mouse," said the little one.

I told you before 'twas a stormy night
When these two little kittens began to fight;
The old woman seized her sweeping broom,
And swept the kittens right out of the room.

The ground was covered with frost and snow,
And the two little kittens had nowhere to go;
So they laid them down on the mat at the door,
While the old woman finished sweeping the floor.

Then they crept in, as quiet as mice,
All wet with the snow, and as cold as ice.
For they found it was better, that stormy night,
To lie down and sleep than to quarrel and fight.

Pussycat, Pussycat

Pussycat, Pussycat, where have you been?
I've been to London to visit the queen.
Pussycat, Pussycat, what did you do there?
I frightened a little mouse under her chair.

The Kitten at Play

See the kitten on the wall,
Sporting with the leaves that fall.

Withered leaves, one, two, and three
Falling from the elder tree.

Through the calm and frosty air
Of the morning bright and fair.

See the kitten, how she starts,
Crouches, stretches, paws and darts;
With a tiger-leap halfway,
Now she meets her coming prey,
Lets it go as fast and then
Has it in her power again.

Now she works with three or four,
Like a graceful juggler;
Quick as he in feats of art,
Gracefully she plays her part;
Yet were gazing thousands there,
What would little Tabby care?

Kitty Cat and the Dumplings

Kitty cat ate the dumplings, the dumplings,
Kitty cat ate the dumplings.
Mama stood by, and cried, "Oh my!
Why did you eat the dumplings?"

Mother Cat

There was a mother cat,
Who ate a ball of yarn,
And when she had kittens,
They all had sweaters on.

Sing, Sing

Sing, sing! What shall I sing?
The cat's run away with my shoestring.
Do, do, what shall I do?
The cat has bit it quite in two.

The Cat and the Fiddle

Hey, diddle, diddle,
The cat and the fiddle,
The cow jumped
Over the moon.
The little dog laughed
To see such sport,
And the dish ran away
With the spoon.

Ding Dong Bell

Ding dong bell,
Kitty's in the well.
Who put her in?
Little Johnny Green.
Who pulled her out?
Little Tommy Stout.
What a naughty boy was that
To try to soak poor kitty cat,
Who never did him any harm,
And chased the mice in Father's barn.

Big and Little Rhymes

Twinkle, Twinkle, Little Star

Twinkle, twinkle, little star,
How I wonder what you are.
Up above the world so high,
Like a diamond in the sky.
Twinkle, twinkle, little star,
How I wonder what you are!

If All the Seas
Were One Sea

If all the seas were one sea,
What a great sea that would be!
And if all the trees were one tree,
What a great tree that would be!
And if all the axes were one ax,
What a great ax that would be!
And if all the men were one man,
What a great man that would be!
And if the great man took the great ax,
And cut down the great tree,
And let it fall into the great sea,
What a splish-splash that would be!

Little Tommy Tittlemouse

Little Tommy Tittlemouse
Lived in a little house.
He caught fishes
In other men's ditches.

Little Tommy Tittlemouse
Lived in a bellhouse.
The bellhouse broke;
Tommy Tittlemouse awoke.

Little Girl and Queen

Little girl, little girl,
Where have you been?
Gathering roses
To give to the queen.
Little girl, little girl,
What gave she you?
She gave me a diamond
As big as my shoe.

The Giant Jim

The giant Jim, great giant grim,
Wears a hat without a brim,
Weighs a ton, and wears a blouse,
And trembles when he meets a mouse.

Jerry Hall

Jerry Hall,
He is so small,
A rat could eat him,
Hat and all.

Little Ships

Little ships

Must keep the shore;

Larger ships

May venture more.

The Little Nut Tree

I had a little nut tree.
Nothing would it bear
But a silver nutmeg,
And a golden pear.
The King of Spain's daughter
Came to visit me,
And all for the sake
Of my little nut tree.

Little Tee Wee

Little Tee Wee,
He went to sea
In an open boat.

And while afloat,
The little boat bended,
And my story's ended.

Bedtime Rhymes

Sleep Tight

Good night,
Sleep tight,
Don't let the bedbugs bite.

Wee Willie Winkie

Wee Willie Winkie
Runs through the town,
Upstairs and downstairs
In his nightgown,
Rapping at the window,
Crying through the lock,
"Are the children all in bed?
Now it's eight o'clock."

Sleep, Baby, Sleep

Sleep, baby, sleep.
Your father guards the sheep.
Your mother shakes
The dreamland tree,
And from it fall
Sweet dreams for thee.
Sleep, baby, sleep.

Rock-a-Bye, Baby

Rock-a-bye, baby,
On the treetop.
When the wind blows,
The cradle will rock.
When the bough breaks,
The cradle will fall.
Down will come baby,
Cradle and all.

Bedtime

The evening is coming,
The sun sinks to rest;

The rooks are all flying
Straight home to the nest.

"Caw!" says the rook, as he flies overhead;
"It's time little people were going to bed!"

The Cock Crows

The cock crows in the morn
To tell us to rise,
And he that lies late
Will never be wise:
For early to bed
And early to rise
Is the way to be healthy
And wealthy and wise.

Diddle, Diddle, Dumpling

Diddle, diddle, dumpling,
My son John
Went to bed with his trousers on;
One shoe off, and one shoe on,
Diddle, diddle, dumpling,
My son John.

Sleepy Cat

The cat sat asleep
By the side of the fire.
The mistress snored loud as a pig.

John took up his fiddle,
By Jenny's desire,
And struck up a bit of a jig.

The Moon

The moon has a face like a clock in the hall;
She shines on thieves on the garden wall,
On streets and fields and harbor quays,
And birdies asleep in the forks of the trees.

The squalling cat and the squeaking mouse,
The howling dog by the door of the house,
The bat that lies in bed at noon,
All love to be out by the light of the moon.

Come, Let's to Bed

Come, let's to bed, says Sleepyhead.
Sit up awhile, says Slow.
Hang on the pot, says Greedy-gut,
We'll sup before we go.

To bed, to bed, cried Sleepyhead,
But all the rest said no!
It's morning now; you must milk the cow,
And tomorrow to bed we go.

Lullaby and Good Night

Lullaby and good night,
Put your head down and sleep tight.
Lie down now and rest;
May your slumber be blessed.

Index